JACOB'S NEW DRESS

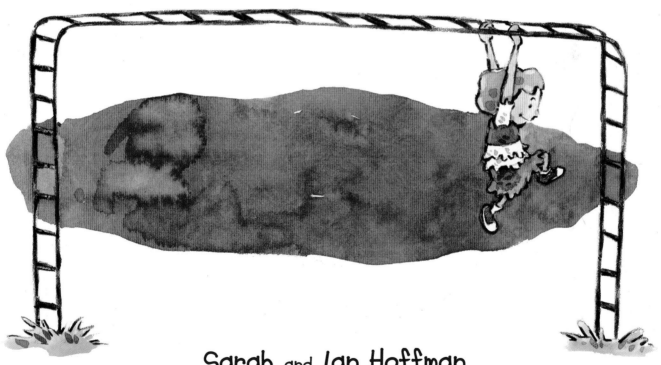

Sarah and Ian Hoffman

illustrated by Chris Case

ALBERT WHITMAN & COMPANY
CHICAGO, ILLINOIS

For Sam Hoffman & Patrick Eleey:
our two generations of Jacob—SH and IH

For Olivia, of course—CC

Library of Congress Cataloging-in-Publication Data

Hoffman, Sarah, author.
Jacob's new dress / by Sarah and Ian Hoffman ; illustrated by Chris Case.
pages cm
Summary: Jacob, who likes to wear dresses at home,
convinces his parents to let him wear a dress to school too.
[1. Gender identity—Fiction. 2. Sex role—Fiction.
3. Dresses—Fiction. 4. Clothing and dress—Fiction.]
I. Hoffman, Ian, author. II. Case, Chris, illustrator. III. Title.
PZ7.H67585Jac 2014
[E]—dc23   2013028443

Printed in China
11 10 9 8 7 6 LP 22 21 20 19 18 17

The design is by Nick Tiemersma.

For more information about Albert Whitman & Company,
visit our website at www.albertwhitman.com.

Jacob ran to join Emily in the dress-up corner.

Emily slid into a shiny yellow dress while Jacob wiggled into a sparkly pink dress.

They both reached for the crown, but Jacob got there first.

"I'll be the princess," he said.

Christopher frowned. "Jacob, why do you always wear the girl clothes? Put on the knight armor. That's what the boy wears!"

"Christopher, stop telling us what to do!" said Emily.

Ms. Wilson heard the hubbub.
"What's going on, kids?"
"Jacob is wearing girl clothes!"
complained Christopher.

"The dress-up corner is where we come to use our imaginations," Ms. Wilson said. "You can be a dinosaur, a princess, a farmer—anything! Christopher, what do you want to be?"

"A *boy*." Christopher scowled.

Ms. Wilson smiled. "Jacob, you try it! What new thing could you imagine being? A firefighter? A policeman?"

"Ms. Wilson," Jacob said proudly, "*I'm* the princess."

"How was school today?" Mom asked, studying Jacob's face. "Fun?"

"Christopher says boys can't wear dresses," said Jacob. "Can they?"

"Of course they can." Mom hugged Jacob. "Why don't you get the dress you wore on Halloween and play in that."

Jacob pulled on his witch's dress and twirled. He loved the way the black lace swirled around him.

"I want to wear my dress to school!"

Jacob's mom frowned.

"I don't think so," she said. "That's for dress-up at home. It would get dirty at school."

"Then can I get a regular dress? A dress I can wear to school?"

Mom was quiet.

"Let me think about that," she said.

Jacob wondered what to play next. Pirate? Princess? Bird!

Heaping three towels onto the floor, Jacob made a nest. Then he wrapped another towel around himself for feathers.

Snug and warm, he imagined what a school dress would look like.

The next morning, Jacob stood on the stairs wrapped in a giant bath towel.

"What are you wearing?" asked Mom.

"It's like a dress, but I can get it dirty," Jacob said, pointing to the towel. "I made it!"

Dad frowned. "You can't go to school like that."

"Put on some shorts and a shirt under that dress-thing," Mom said. "And hurry—we're late for school!"

"What's that?" demanded Christopher. Jacob moved closer to his mom.

"Good morning, Christopher," said Jacob's mom. "Jacob's wearing something new he invented. Isn't it nice?"

Christopher didn't answer.

"I want a dress like that!" cried Emily. "Where'd you get it?"

"It's not a dress," said Jacob, glancing up at his mom. "It's a...*dress-thing*." Jacob saw Emily's smile and grinned back. "I can make you one!"

The playground was full of laughter and running feet as the children played tag.

Christopher sneaked up, yanked off Jacob's towel, and ran away whooping.

"Christopher is *mean*," hissed Emily.

Jacob watched Christopher wave the towel like a captured flag and started to cry.

"How was school today?" Mom asked.

"Christopher stole my dress-thing," said Jacob. The tears flooded back.

Mom hugged Jacob. "I'm sorry. Christopher's not always a good friend."

"Mom?" whispered Jacob. "Can you help me make a real dress?"

Mom didn't answer. The longer she didn't answer, the less Jacob could breathe.

"Let's get the sewing machine," she said finally. Jacob felt the air refill his body. He grinned. Mom smiled back.

"There are all sorts of ways to be a boy," she said. "Right?"

Dad looked up from his book.

"Mom and I made a dress," said Jacob quietly.

Dad studied the dress. Jacob started to get that can't-breathe feeling again.

"I can see you worked hard on that dress," said Dad. "Are you sure you want to wear it to school?"

Jacob nodded.

Dad nodded back and smiled. "Well, it's not what I would wear, but you look great."

Jacob skipped up the front walk to school. He found Emily inside and showed her his new dress. They found matching colors in their clothes and laughed: purple and white!

"Do you want to play dress up?" asked Emily.

"No. Monkey bars!"

Together they ran out to the playground.

"My mom and I made this dress!" Jacob said proudly at circle time. "We used her sewing machine!"

"That's wonderful!" said Ms. Wilson. "Was the sewing machine hard to use?"

"Why does Jacob wear dresses?" interrupted Christopher.

Ms. Wilson paused. "I think Jacob wears what he's comfortable in. Just like you do. Not very long ago little girls couldn't wear pants. Can you imagine that?"

Christopher shook his head. "I asked my dad, and he says boys don't wear dresses."

Jacob rubbed the hem of his dress, looking at the little stitches he'd sewn himself. He could hear Ms. Wilson and the other kids talking, but their words sounded far away.

On the playground, Christopher yelled, "Let's play tag! Boys versus girls—Jacob, you're on the *girls* team!"

A bunch of kids laughed.

Jacob felt his dress surrounding him.

Like armor.

Soft, cottony, *magic* armor.

"Christopher, I made this dress, I'm proud of it, and I'm going to wear it!

"And you know what else?" Jacob tagged Christopher. "You're it!"

Jacob sprinted across the playground, his dress spreading out like wings.

When Dr. Edgardo Menvielle and I launched the Gender and Sexuality Advocacy and Education Program in 1998, there was no support network of any kind for the families of gender-nonconforming children. Since then, clinics have opened in several major cities across the United States, along with numerous support groups, both in-person and online. If you're a parent coming to this issue for the first time, getting in touch with a clinic or support group is a great place to start.

As parents, teachers, librarians, and pediatricians, we need to teach that there is nothing wrong with gender nonconformity, just as there is nothing wrong with left-handedness or any other way of being different. Pink boys—like all children—need our support and affirmation to become fully who they are.

Catherine Tuerk, MA, APRN
Senior Consultant, Gender and Sexuality Advocacy and Education Program
Children's National Medical Center, Washington, DC

When our son, Sam, was a preschooler he had long hair, wore dresses, and loved the color pink. Sam also liked traditional "boy" things, like knights, castles, and dinosaurs. Clinically, children like Sam are called gender nonconforming; we liked to call him a pink boy—the male equivalent of a tomboy.

We didn't think there was anything wrong with being a pink boy, but we knew Sam was different—and different isn't always easy. For Sam's sake, we worked hard to educate ourselves about gender-nonconforming children. Gender expression is an important part of every person's identity, and it's inborn—not something we choose. Gender-nonconforming children are often teased and stigmatized for their differences, and research shows their stress levels are higher than those of gender-normative kids. Studies also show that support and acceptance from family, peers, and community make a huge difference in the future health and mental health of these kids.

There is still a lot we don't know—like why some kids are gender-nonconforming. We don't know whether or not a particular child will "grow out" of it. And it's not possible to know whether a gender-nonconforming child will grow up to be gay, straight, bisexual, or transgender. (Actually, we think it's too early to know this about any young child.)

Finding support for Sam—and us—has been essential. *Jacob's New Dress* was born of our commitment to help parents, families, teachers, and physicians stand behind all the differently gendered little people in their lives.

Ian and Sarah Hoffman

To Dom and Shabs the cat

First published 2018 by Two Hoots
an imprint of Pan Macmillan
20 New Wharf Road, London N1 9RR
Associated companies throughout the world
www.panmacmillan.com
ISBN 978-1-5098-3799-1

Text and illustrations copyright © Polly Dunbar 2018

Moral rights asserted.

3 5 7 9 8 6 4 2
A CIP catalogue record for this book is available from the British Library.
Printed in China

The illustrations in this book were created with a Rotring ink pen, pencil,
crayons, felt tip pens, watercolour paint and a little bit of Photoshop.

www.twohootsbooks.com

Something Fishy

Polly Dunbar

TWO HOOTS

Hello.

I am a cat.

And like all cats . . .

I love fish.

This is my family. I love them, too.

They give me lots of fish.

Hmm.
Something fishy
is going on.

But not in a good way.

Hang on . . .

wait . . .

Here comes the fish now.

You ARE joking.

I ask for one

simple

thing . . .

And THIS
is what I get.

Sheesh.

Perhaps if I ask really nicely.

Can I have some fish purrleease?

Here it comes. The BIG FISH SURPRISE . . .

Oh, you've decorated my room.

How nice.

And a new cat basket?

Wonderful.

But . . .

WHERE IS THE FISH?

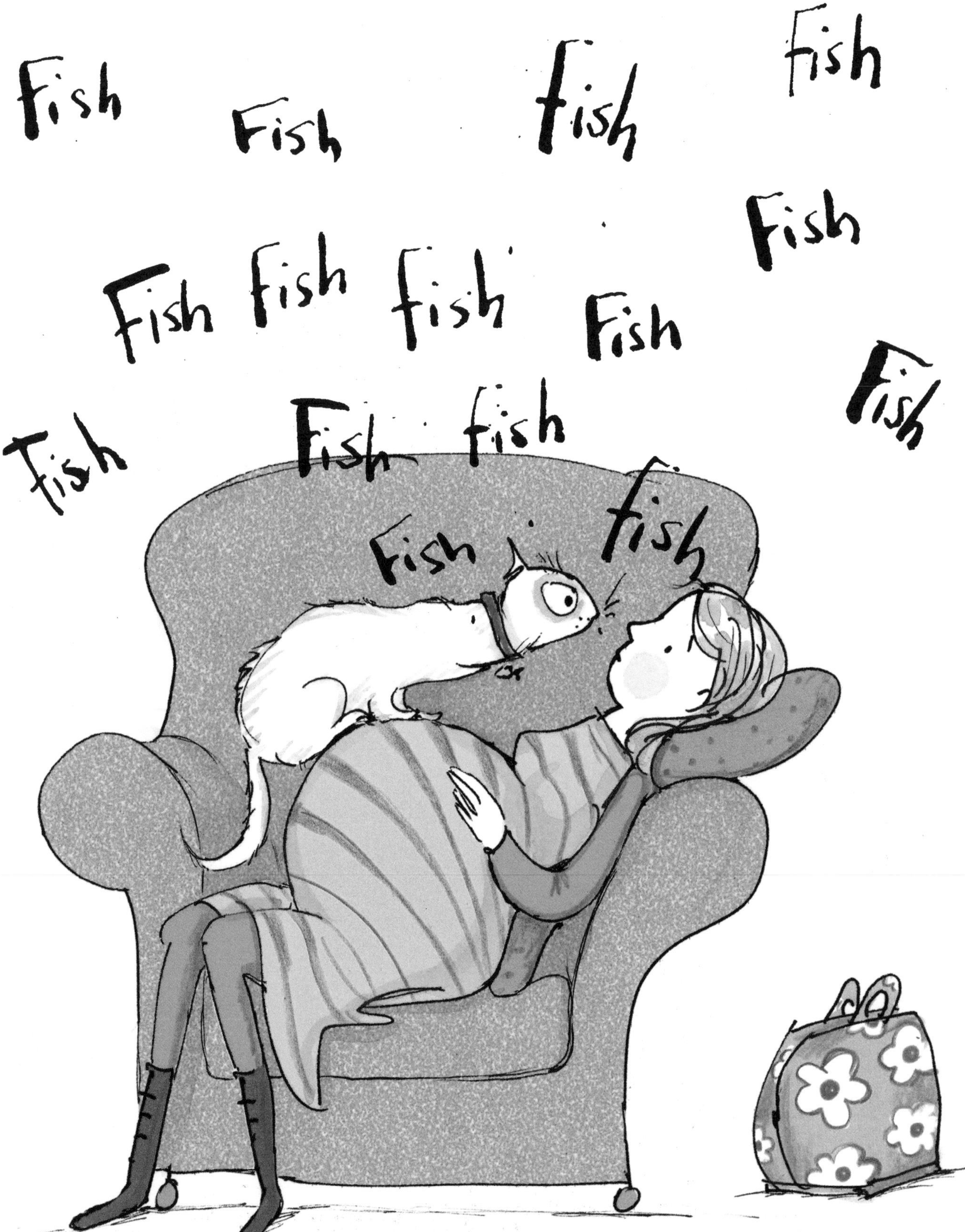

Oh.

They've gone.

Gone . . .

Gone . . .

Gone FISHING!

Of
course!

To catch the swishiest

squishiest

fishiest fish.

I lick my lips and

wish for . . .

Oh no.

NOT

THIS!

This . . .

is NOT . . .

FISH.

Hang on.
Wait.

Could it
really be . . .

FISH!

In

my

dish.

Mmm . . .

delish.

This is my family, and
I love them.

Even if . . .

I have
to put up with
THIS.

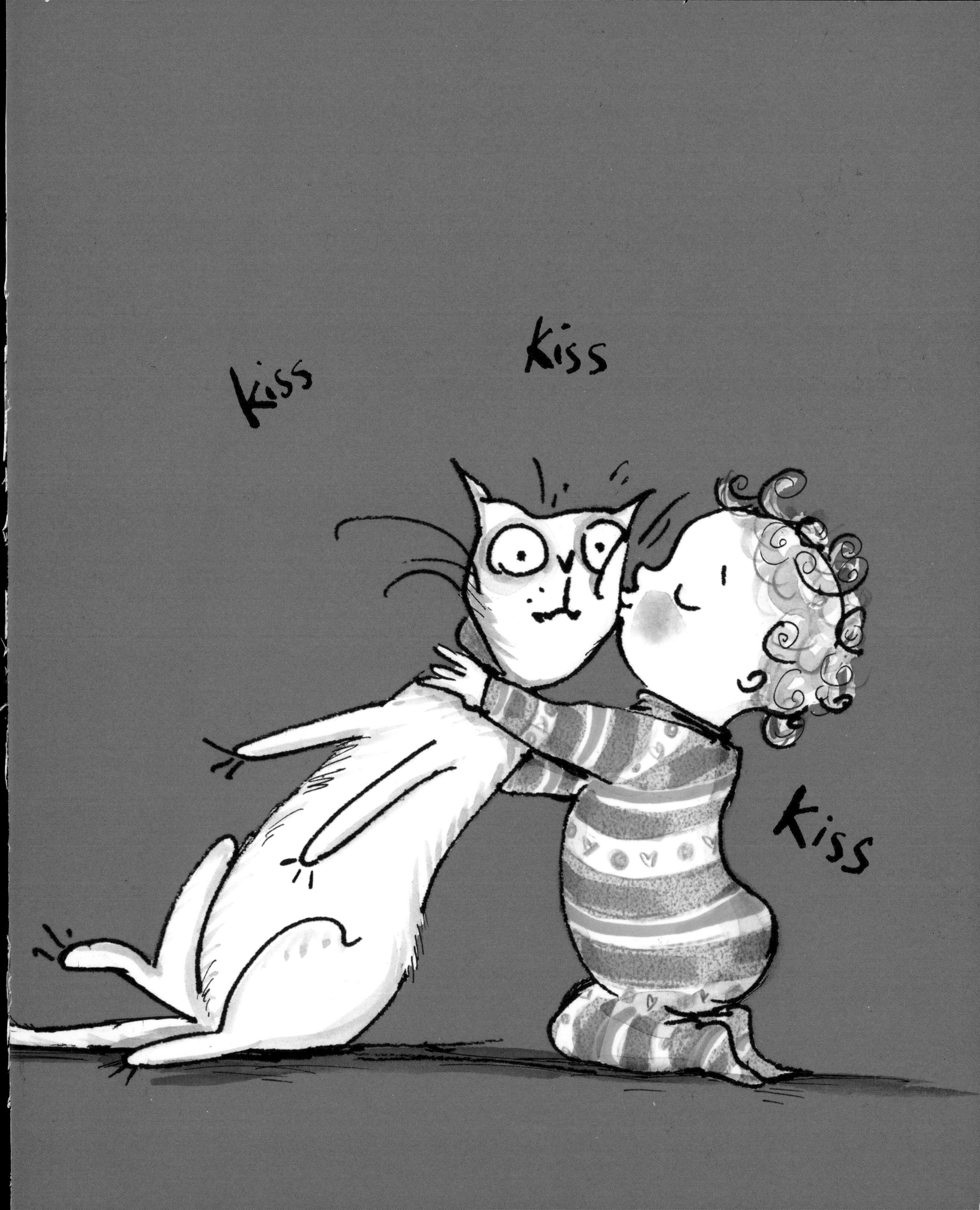
kiss
kiss
kiss